THE 24TH NAME
Part II

by

John Braddock

For updates on next books, join John's
email list at:

www.spysguide.com

ISBN: 9781092403412

CONTENTS

Chapter 1

I thought the attack would come on Day Five.

Which meant a bunch of things would happen between Days One and Four.

The first thing was that Angelo would tell his father what happened in Florida.

That would be on Day Two, because I thought Day One would be Angelo nursing his broken nose and deciding whether to tell his father what I did. But Angelo would tell his father what I did because the sober home racket in the Florida beach town was shut down, Roger was hospitalized, and the Cuban killer had seen me. The hurt on the business plus the Cuban as a witness meant Angelo needed to blame someone. He would blame me on Day Two.

When he did that, a second thing would happen on Day Two: Angelo's father would decide whether to:

1. Come after me; or
2. Not to come after me.

Most criminals would choose Option 2: They'd leave me alone. They knew I could defend myself. They knew I could cause damage. And since I'd left Florida, I wasn't causing any more trouble. My home was in Wisconsin, as far as they knew. Which was a good distance from Florida. And a good distance from upstate New York, where Jake and I ran into them the first time. Most people would choose Option 2.

But some people have a different mindset. You could call it a survival mindset. Or a vengeance mindset. Or a Zero-Sum mindset.

Whatever you call it, it's the mindset that

obsesses on enemies. The mindset that says you should destroy anyone who attacks you.

That mindset would want to kill me for what I'd done to Angelo and his business in Florida. Which is why I'd given them Jake's name. So they would come to Wisconsin, in case they had the mindset that would choose Option 1.

If Angelo's father chose Option 1, Day Three would be a mustering, planning and logistics day for his men. On Day Four, the men would arrive at Jake's cabin in Wisconsin and do reconnaissance. Which meant the attack would come on Day Five.

When they attacked, I'd separate one from the group. I'd ask him why the Cubans had been in upstate New York. I'd ask him why they were using the weapons of Quebecois separatists. I'd ask why they panicked and killed Bill, the gun range owner. And I'd be a step closer to fixing the injustice of killing Jake.

But that all depended on me being right about the things that would happen between

Days One and Four.

I was probably wrong about one of those things. Maybe, two. Or maybe I was wrong about the most fundamental thing: Maybe Angelo's father didn't have the Zero-Sum mindset.

It turned out I was wrong about even more.

And I was wrong about how many would come after me.

Instead of a group, there was one.

Fortunately, I saw him before he saw me.

Chapter 2

My fifth name was for a nuclear bombmaker.

It was a brand-new name, so the CIA told me to choose it.

When the CIA tells you to choose a new name, they tell you to choose a name unconnected to you, which isn't easy.

Our minds are built on connections. Our memories are linked to other memories. Our thoughts are connected to other thoughts. Our minds thrive on connections.

Our minds make connections in three ways, according to David Hume:

1. Through resemblance
2. By contiguity in time or place, and
3. Due to cause and effect.

Which is useful, most of the time.

It's useful to find things that resemble each other, because things that resemble each other usually act the same. If two balls look alike and we see one bounce, chances are the other one will bounce the same way.

It's useful to find contiguity, so we know what to expect next in time or place. If something happens just before something else, the first thing may have caused the second thing. If something sits next to something else, chances are those two things are connected in some way.

Then, there are causes and effects. Causes and effects and the connections between them are what our minds are always trying to figure out.

Resemblance, contiguity and cause and effect help us make predictions about what happens next.

Which is a problem when you're a spy.

When you're a spy, you don't want to be

connected as a cause to the effects that are happening. You don't want contiguity of time or place to bombs going off or sources being recruited or cryptography being stolen. And you don't want a resemblance to how people think of spies. You don't want anything connecting you to being a spy.

One way to break those connections is to use a new name. A name unconnected to you. A name unconnected to the CIA. A name that breaks the connection between you and the espionage that's about to happen.

But that's hard. It's hard to come up with something that doesn't resemble you and isn't contiguous to you and isn't connected to you via cause or effect.

To create something unconnected, a new data source helps.

Like a book.

Books take you out of your connections and experience. They introduce you to things that don't resemble what you've seen before. They move you out of the contiguity of time and place. They show you new causes and effects. The best books connect you to a whole new way of thinking.

But I didn't need a new way of thinking. I just needed a new name.

So I went to a different data source: Baseball rosters.

I went to the sports page of the local newspaper and chose the last name of a player from the night before. He was a relief pitcher who threw one inning, got one strikeout, gave up two hits and didn't allow any earned runs. More importantly, he had an ordinary last name that wasn't too common: Middleton.

Then I went to the opposing team and chose the first name of the second baseman. He went two for four that day with a double. More importantly, his first name was also ordinary but not too common: Zach.

I went to the online white pages and searched for Zach Middleton. Nationwide, there were 81 Zach Middletons in a country of 300-plus million. Eighty-one was a good number. It was too many to be able to call each one up and see if they were me. And it was too few to make it likely someone in a foreign country would be already connected to a Zach Middleton. Eighty-one was a good number for a brand-new name.

I gave the name to the people who create the paperwork. They did their check for whether Zach Middleton was connected to the CIA in the past.

The answer was no.

Zach Middleton was not connected to the CIA.

And Zach Middleton was not connected to me.

I became the eighty-second Zach Middleton registered in the United States at that time and got ready to use the name with a nuclear bombmaker.

The bombmaker had expertise in the early

stages of building a nuclear weapon. He traveled throughout the Middle East. He knew who was doing what in other nuclear programs. Which meant he was useful to us.

He was young and, from his emails, a little naïve.

I floated an opportunity for him, and he agreed to meet me in Abu Dhabi.

When the paperwork was done and my fifth name was ready, I as Zach Middleton went to meet the nuclear bombmaker.

Chapter 3

After breaking Angelo's nose and leaving the money for Hannah's mom and saying good-bye to Carly, the rest of my Day One was driving. While Angelo was nursing his broken nose and deciding whether to tell his father what happened in Florida, I was on the highways.

It's a long way from Florida to Jake's cabin in Wisconsin. I made it a little longer by going wide around Atlanta, Nashville and Chicago so the big city traffic cameras wouldn't see me. I didn't think anyone was looking for me, but that was just a hypothesis. And, I didn't want enemies I made later to look back through photos and videos and find I had driven from Florida to Wisconsin on Day One.

Whenever I stopped for gas, I found a big box store and bought a motion-sensitive camera with cash. By the time I pulled into the small town near Jake's house, I had five cameras bought in four different states.

I hadn't spent much time in Jake's town since taking his identity. There had been the time when I had my picture taken at the local DMV. The bored DMV lady looked at the documentation and looked at me and told me I looked better without the mustache Jake had in his original driver's license picture. My new driver's license arrived via mail three weeks later.

It was in those three weeks that I wrote my first book, if you can call it that.

The book was short. Very short. But that's how I reached my target audience: Desperate people.

I put the book on an online retailer and let a few people know about it. The title had "spy" and "thinking" in it, so it hit the right keywords.

I priced it low, so a lot of people downloaded it. I didn't put the Digital Rights Management watermarks on it, so it got pirated and spread even more widely.

It was short enough to read in one sitting because desperate people don't have time for long, convoluted books. They need a way to solve their problems quickly. So I gave it to them in a short book. Short enough that they read it and got to the end quickly. Getting to the end was important, because the end was where I put my contact information.

A lot of people read my book. Some of them wrote and asked for help.

My first client was a hotel manager in New Hampshire. He was hundreds of miles from upstate New York, but I had to start somewhere, and Jake was right about me being soft. I needed the practice, so I went to New Hampshire.

The hotel manager hosted illegal poker games run by a wannabe gangster. Which was no big deal until the manager's 11-year-old son was propositioned by one of the whales and the gangster wanted the hotel manager to comply. It didn't take me long to solve the problem. The result was a dead whale, which didn't make the wannabe gangster happy. Who turned into a dead wannabe gangster. The hotel manager was thankful.

Before I left New Hampshire, I gave the hotel manager an envelope and told him not to open it until I called. In return for my services, I told him someday he'd need to help me.

He agreed and became the first member of my new network.

The next client was a real estate agent in Syracuse, which was closer to where Jake died. The real estate agent had learned something about money laundering that she shouldn't have. A couple of lawyers who became state lawmakers had the state police and most of the local authorities doing muscle work for them. Lawyers like to fight in courts where only bailiffs have guns, and even dirty cops are careful about weapons discharges, which make them hold back. Which also make them easier to beat. When it was over, I left her an envelope with the same instructions, and she became the second member of my network.

After Syracuse, the softness was gone. Which was important for what happened next.

When a construction worker in upstate New York emailed for help, I thought I'd found the guys who killed Jake. The construction worker was part of a smuggling operation across the Canadian border and said he wanted out. Some of his story didn't make sense, but I went because I thought Jake's killers were right around the corner.

It turned out to be a set up. The construction worker had seen too many spy movies and wanted to prove he was tougher than an ex-spy. He wasn't. Neither were the four guys from the MMA gym he brought with him.

After that, I was wondering if the book and

network-building was going to work. My network was small, and I wasn't getting connected to the right nodes. I wasn't finding the right people. I was going to try another way to figure out who killed Jake in upstate New York when Hannah's mom reached out.

Florida was even further away from upstate New York, but that's where I found the strand from Angelo's father's business to the guns of the Quebecois separatists. Florida is where I got closer to the people who killed Jake. Florida is where I found a node.

Now, they were going to meet me in Jake's town on Day Five, if my hypotheses were correct.

The morning of Day Two, I pulled on to Jake's street and found a car in his driveway.

Chapter 4

When I as Zach Middleton arrived in Dubai, it was the middle of the night. With the time difference and the flight distance and the preference people have for leaving home during daylight hours, the middle of the night was when a lot of flights arrived in Dubai.

The airport hummed. Jewelry shops and electronic shops were doing business. The prices were stated in the Western way, but buying and selling were done in the Arab way. Haggling and arm waves and walking away and returning was happening everywhere. The floors and walls and stairways glowed brighter than real gold.

You can't be average everywhere. In Dubai, I didn't look like anyone else. And I was alone, which was unlike everyone else. Arabs and Asians and Europeans were in groups. Even the Americans who were ethnically Arab, Asian and European were in twos and threes. I was alone and didn't look average. Two strikes against me. Two reasons for the Border Police to question me.

But they didn't. They let me through with a swipe of my false passport and a glance at my real face. There were no biometric checks in those days. No fingerprints done. No DNA swabbed. Not even a picture taken. Just like that, I as Zach Middleton was through.

I didn't want to be seen by anyone who knew me by one of my four previous names, so I went right to the taxi stand and got in line.

The line was a dozen people long. Halfway to the front was a dark, bearded man alone like me. He was looking around in a nonchalant, observant way. He was unlike the businesspeople. He was unlike the families on vacation. He wasn't focused on his luggage or the taxi line or the cars passing by. He was focused on the whole environment.

He was aware.

When he got to the front of the line, he put his suitcase in the back seat with him, and the taxi driver sped off.

That's when I saw the surveillance.

It must have been the local security service because two unmarked cars in no parking zones pulled out to follow. I looked for who had told them to do it and saw a man standing by a pillar twenty yards away. He was watching the cars go and touching his ear like he was listening.

It was unlikely there were two surveillance teams, and even more unlikely that they would have followed me, since I had a new name. But just to be sure, when it was my turn to get in the taxi, I told the driver to take me by the indoor ski resort on the way to Abu Dhabi.

"It's closed," he said, which was true, since it was the middle of the night.

"I know, but I want to see how big it is up close," I said. I gave him an extra bill and he nodded.

This was before the Burj and the artificial islands, but of the five biggest cranes in the world, four were in Dubai. Ridiculous things were going up fast. Someone told me that if you had half a thought about something that would bring more people to Dubai, the construction started. They were throwing ideas and buildings against the blank canvas of the desert to see what stuck. I watched behind the taxi as we took a couple of turns. By the time we got to the indoor ski resort, I was satisfied no one had followed us. I told the taxi driver to take me to Abu Dhabi.

Abu Dhabi is technically an island, but right there on the coast, separated by little rivers and joined to the mainland by bridges.

At that time, it was much smaller than Dubai. It had just a few high rises, including the hotel I was staying in next to a five-story mall.

I had told the nuclear bombmaker to meet me in that mall a few hours after the sun rose.

When I got to the hotel, it was too late to sleep and too early to go to the mall, so I grabbed a coffee at the lobby bar and sat by the front window. Late arrivers and early risers passed through the doors and milled in the lobby. After a while, I could tell the locals from the visitors and the businesspeople from the plainclothes security officers watching everyone. I felt the rhythm of the place.

When it was time, I went to the Abu Dhabi mall to meet the nuclear bombmaker.

Chapter 5

The night before I pulled on to Jake's street, it rained. Some of the wet rocks behind the car in his driveway had their dry side turned up, which meant the car hadn't been there overnight.

The car was an older small four-door sedan. On the trunk were cloudy, chalky splotches where the paint had worn away from too much Wisconsin snow or too much Wisconsin sun or too many Wisconsin days that went from sun to snow. On the back window was a fancy monogram with the letters SGB. I drove past the driveway and parked around a turn in the road.

I pulled a Glock from the foot well and jogged toward Jake's house.

Jake's house was an A-frame built out of logs. Facing the road was a garage with the door closed. On the other side, a deck faced a lake.

I didn't think the car in Jake's driveway was a risk, but I wanted to be sure. I pulled the passenger door open and fished around in the glove box until I found an insurance card and state registration issued to Sarah B. Grimes.

I knew the name but hadn't met her. She was the housecleaner paid each month out of Jake's bank account. Which meant there would be no problem, if she was alone.

To be sure she was alone, I circled behind the garage and stepped around scrub brushes growing through wet leaves.

Under a window, I heard a muffled hum inside in the house. A few steps further, and I was at the deck. No one was on it, so I went back to the window and looked inside.

A woman was vacuuming. It wasn't loud, but that's because houses in Wisconsin are well-sealed against the cold of winter. I didn't see anyone else, so I went back to the door facing the driveway. As soon as the vacuum stopped, I turned the keys in the lock and opened the door.

A woman in her early thirties looked up from wrapping the vacuum cord. She had dusty blond hair tied back and pale skin with freckles high on her cheeks. Around her mouth and eyes were light creases. She looked at me like she might know me, which is the effect of being mostly average.

But she didn't know me. Or Jake, either. Because she looked at the keys in my hand and said, "Mr. Beamer? Welcome home." She went to the window and looked at the driveway. "My car's not in your way, is it? Where's your car?"

"A friend dropped me off," I said. "Thanks for getting everything clean. It's Sarah, right?"

Sarah nodded. "You're welcome. It's easy. Were you even here since the last time I cleaned? It wasn't dirty."

I smiled. "I like things really clean. Do I owe you a check?"

She looked at me sideways. "No, you mailed me one last week."

"Right," I smiled. "It's set up automatically at the bank."

She looked at me sideways again and said, "I don't want to say you're overpaying me, but if you're not going to be here, there's not much to clean."

The way she said it, it was like I'd done something wrong. Like me not being there and her cleaning was a mistake I had made. And she expected me to apologize for it. But I hadn't done anything wrong, so I didn't apologize.

Instead, I said, "How do you want to fix it? Should I pay you less next time?"

She smiled and said, "No. How about I take you to lunch, and we call it even?"

There were no rings on Sarah's left hand, and I had two more days before Angelo's father's men arrived, if my hypotheses were right. So I said, "Not dinner?"

"You didn't overpay me that much," Sarah said. "Lunch should be enough. The diner on Main at noon?"

That gave me two hours to set up the cameras, so I said, "Sounds good."

"I'll be done in five minutes."

"I'll wait on the deck," I said because it didn't seem right to be in the house while she was working.

From the deck, Jake's land sloped to a floating wooden dock. Beyond the dock was a fifty-acre lake with shorelines rough enough to not be manmade. Thirty yards out, a fish broke the surface and sent widening circles away. On the far shore, the last of the morning's fog rose through green and yellow cattails.

It was a relaxing scene. A beautiful scene. The kind of scene you could get used to.

Which I was tempted to do. With Jake's name and ID and property, it would be easy to sit on this deck and go down to the dock each day and watch fish break the surface. It'd be easy to watch the fog rising and the sun setting and the other beautiful things I hadn't seen yet. It would be easy to find a woman like Sarah, if not Sarah herself, and get used to this place.

Which is what Jake must have felt. He must have felt the same way on the same deck when he looked at the same dock on the same lake and met the same kind of woman. He must have felt the pull of mornings where the scene was so beautiful, you understood the meaning of the world.

Which a guy like Jake couldn't let happen. He had a craving for conflict. A desire to be in places and situations and fights where you come through or you don't. Which is why Jake built a network of retired Marines. Which is why he went everywhere looking for the right people to fight for. And the right enemies to fight.

No wonder he didn't spend much time here.

If you stare too long at a beautiful lake like that, you're going to get soft. Worse, you're going to want to get soft. Which for Jake wasn't really a decision. At least, not a conscious one.

For me, it was different. I didn't have Jake's craving for conflict. I didn't have his desire for places and situation and fights where you come through or you don't. I didn't need enemies.

But I was like him in other ways. I'd been trained and conditioned and built to do things in certain ways. To take the data I gathered, analyze it, decide, and take action. To take action, I would become what the job needed.

Now, the job was to find the guys who killed Jake. Because someone had to find them. Someone had to stop whatever they were doing that was important enough to kill Jake.

To do that, I had become what was needed to find Jake's killers.

Or attract them, like I hoped I'd done.

Chapter 6

The world of nuclear bombmakers is like baseball: Even the top players start off in the minor leagues. They learn their craft and build expertise in a developmental program. Maybe the program is run by a government, or maybe it's a university with a nuclear reactor. In the program, developing nuclear bombmakers get practice on real-world equipment with real-world isotopes and learn the fundamentals. That's when the assessments start.

In baseball, scouts grade major league prospects in at least five categories. There's speed, hitting for average, hitting for power, fielding ability and throwing ability. The best players have them all, and they're called "Five-tool players." Which means they have a skill stack, like Hall of Famers Willie Mays, Alex Rodriquez and Hank Aaron. They combine all five "tools" together to become great.

Then, there are the Lenny Dykstras of baseball. They have one or two "tools," but manage to make it in the major leagues with hard work and hustle.

I didn't know how many tools this nuclear bombmaker had. He was young and still developing. No one knew if he would become a major league player, but he was ambitious and hard-working and ready to hustle, which is why he had agreed to meet me in Abu Dhabi.

And that's why I went to meet him in Abu Dhabi: I was a scout trying to figure out how many tools he had, and how many more he could develop. I wanted to see if he was going to play in the major leagues of nuclear bombmaking. More importantly, if he was going to be in the major leagues, if he would be my source. He was a hot prospect.

In baseball, word gets around about the hot

prospects. Other scouts hear things about a player, and soon you have two or three or more scouts watching the same guy.

The same can happen with developing nuclear bombmakers.

The Abu Dhabi mall was five stories tall, and I had told the nuclear bombmaker to meet me at an ice cream shop on the second floor.

Above the second-floor ice cream shop was a third-floor coffee shop with windows over the mall entrance. From there, I could watch him enter. He'd go to the open middle where escalators stretched up and down. The walk and escalator ride would put him in view for about thirty seconds, if he didn't run up the escalator.

Thirty seconds isn't much, but it would give me time to judge his demeanor. Was he nervous? Was he worried? Was he under stress? Was he sweating like he had a bomb strapped around his chest?

A couple of minutes before our meeting

time, I saw the nuclear bombmaker come through the mall doors.

It would take him a few seconds to get to the escalators below me, so I got up to get in position. But I turned and glanced one more time at the street below. That's when I saw it.

Two guys jumped out of a black Mercedes. It was the kind of Mercedes that everyone has in the Middle East, so it wasn't the Mercedes that caught my eye. It was the way they jumped out and sprinted ten steps to the mall entrance. Then, right before the door, they slowed down. One of them pulled open the door and they both walked casually into the mall.

When a surveillance team is on someone, their primary job is to make sure the target doesn't see them. To do that, they act normal while their target is near. They walk at a normal pace. They blend in.

But when the target is out of sight, surveillance teams don't act normal. They make hand signals to other surveillants. They sprint ahead to get in position. Or they stop. They pause for no reason. Maybe, they touch their ear and listen to an earpiece.

When you're doing countersurveillance, you look for what surveillants do when they're not near their target. You watch for what happens after their target passes by.

I went to the open area over the escalators and watched them from the third floor.

With a hand signal, one told the other to stay on the first floor. The one who gave the instruction rode the escalator to the second floor.

I compared the surveillant's face to the picture in my mind of the surveillant at the airport. No resemblance. And we weren't connected to that place by contiguity of time or place. And there were no cause and effect relationships between what I'd seen at the airport and what was happening now.

No connection.

No connection between the airport

surveillants and this one, that I could tell. But surveillants operate in teams, sometimes twenty or more people. He could have been a member of the team that I hadn't seen.

By that time, the nuclear bombmaker was sitting in the ice cream shop looking around. When the surveillant got to the top of the escalator, the bombmaker looked at him to see if he was me. The surveillant ignored the bombmaker and went to a clothing store where he could watch behind glass and mannequins. Where he could see who the nuclear bombmaker would meet.

Who was supposed to be me.

I stayed on the third floor and watched through the steel-topped glass barrier. I waited twenty minutes. The bombmaker waited twenty minutes. Finally, he glanced at his watch and left.

When he did, he went back down the escalator. The surveillant on the first floor followed him out the mall door. The surveillant in the clothing store emerged a moment later and followed.

The bombmaker was under surveillance. But I didn't know why.

Still, I had a series of decisions to make about what happened next.

But I made a mistake.

I didn't go one level further.

I didn't ask myself whether someone was watching me watch the surveillants.

Chapter 7

To set a good tripwire, it should be:

1. Difficult to get around (to avoid false negatives); and

2. Where the wrong people won't trip it (to avoid false positives).

A good place to set a tripwire is a low-traffic chokepoint.

A chokepoint is a natural funnel of traffic. It could be a bridge or a tunnel or a mountain pass. It could be a one lane road. Or the only entrance to a street.

There was only one entrance to Jake's street. And it was four hundred yards from his house, which meant it did the third thing needed for a good tripwire: It gave me time to react.

I didn't know what time of day or night they would come, but I needed at least fifteen seconds to get ready. Four hundred yards gave me at least twenty seconds the first time they came, because the first time they came, they'd go slow.

The entrance to Jake's street did all three things you need in a good tripwire. It was so good, I wondered if Jake had chosen the house because of it.

From Jake's driveway, I couldn't see the two houses between Jake's house and the entrance. They were empty, with garages closed, which meant they were probably summer homes locked up for the coming winter. But it was good they were there because Angelo's father's men would need to go slow past them to be sure they found the right one.

Further down Jake's street were five more houses, but only two had people living in them, which meant the rest were summer homes, too.

When I drove to the end of the street, there were a total of four cars in driveways and in front of houses and inside an open garage. Which meant four possible false positives for the tripwire I would set up, plus a couple of cars that weren't home during the day. Plus the mail truck and deliveries and visitors and repair people and house cleaners like Sarah.

But deliveries wouldn't come every day. And houses don't need repairs every day. And I was probably the only one who had a house cleaner. On any given day, I estimated ten to twelve cars would enter Jake's street. Which wasn't too many false positives.

When I set up the camera by the entrance, I put it back in the trees and high enough kids walking by wouldn't see it and couldn't reach it. The camera was motion-sensitive and connected to the local cellular network. I tested it by walking down the road. An alert with video of me walking on the road appeared on my phone.

Three cameras went around the house. The first showed the view from the door toward the gravel driveway. The second was on the garage facing the road. The third was above the deck toward the lake. I didn't think an attack would come from the lake, but that was just a hypothesis.

With four cameras set and tested and one held in reserve, I got Jake's weapons ready.

In his basement, Jake had an arsenal. He had rifles, shotguns and pistols in most calibers. But to keep things simple, I wanted one caliber, so I grabbed two Glocks and a short-barrel 9mm rifle with a lower receiver cut for Glock magazines. The bullets are single-stacked instead of double-stacked in a Glock magazine. That makes the magazines longer and skinnier when they're high-capacity, which was also better for concealment. But the main advantage was simplicity. When the shooting started, I didn't want to grab the wrong magazine.

Jake had cleaned and oiled the weapons, and I had cleaned and oiled them, but I cleaned and oiled them and tested the actions again.

I didn't know exactly who would come after me, but I had to imagine someone, so I imagined the guys would be like the Cuban who killed Rick. Former soldiers, with no problem killing. Guys who followed orders. Guys who could be patient. Guys who got the job done efficiently and with the minimum of risk, so they could move on to the next job.

With them in mind, I decided to set up the fifth camera by the entrance to the road, but across the road and at a different angle. Then, I went back to the first camera by the road entrance and buried one of the Glocks under a tree.

After that, it was time to meet Sarah for lunch.

Chapter 8

When I got back to my hotel room in Abu Dhabi, I set up the VPN and sat down to write the nuclear bombmaker an email.

Before I could, someone knocked at the door.

When you're a spy in alias in a hotel room in a foreign country, you don't like knocks on your door.

You don't like it because it means one of four things. It's either:

1. Housekeeping; or
2. Hotel management; or
3. The police; or
4. Someone who wants you dead.

The best-case scenario was housekeeping, and it was also the most likely. But I had checked in just eight hours before, so it was odd that housekeeping was at the room already.

The second most likely knocker was hotel management with a billing problem, but they probably would have called first. The third most likely was the police, but I hadn't done anything dumb like buy alcohol to get their attention.

The least likely possibility was someone who wanted me dead. The probability was near zero, because it was unlikely someone who wanted me dead knew I was at this hotel in a new alias. But risk management also tells you to prevent the worst first. If it's a possibility higher than zero, and the consequence is death, you take care of that first.

So I did something simple: I put a book to the peephole.

I put a book to the peephole because the

best way to kill is by surprise. And the best way to kill someone after knocking on their door is to shoot through the peephole when it darkens. You shoot out the peephole, and the bullet follows the glass and the metal from the peephole into the brain.

I didn't want that to happen to me, so I stood to the side and put the book to the peephole.

Nothing happened.

A few seconds later, a second knock came, and I looked through the peephole.

A housekeeper's cart and the side of a woman's face was in view.

She took out a keycard and got ready to unlock the door.

I opened the door.

I was expecting an apology or a "I'll come back later" or a conversation, but there were no words. She took a step toward me and pushed me in the chest. I wasn't expecting it, so I was off balance and went two steps back. She pulled the cart into the room, shut the door behind her, and pulled out a gun.

I'm a little quicker than average. When I saw the gun coming up, I knocked it away out of instinct. Before I realized I'd done it. Before I thought about the gun or asked myself why she was pointing it at me.

I just did it.

The gun flew into the bathroom and chipped a piece of floor tile.

She didn't seem to mind.

She raised her hands in front of her face with the palms flat. Not balled up in fists. Flat, with her thumbs tight against her fingers.

Like she was going to fight me.

That's when I realized I didn't know how to fight a woman.

Chapter 9

The diner on Main Street had large windows. Above eye level were signs advertising homemade buttermilk pancakes, early bird breakfast specials, all-you-can-eat fish on Fridays and all-you-can-eat ham on Sundays.

I got there ten minutes before noon. Sarah wasn't there yet, so I took a window booth facing the door. Cars went by outside and people entered. I let the license plates and vehicle types and how people walked and the way they greeted each other seep in. I was watching for what was normal in Jake's hometown. So when outsiders came, I would see them right away.

The waitress came by and looked at me like she knew me. Which happens a lot when you're mostly average. "You from here?" she asked.

"I've got a place outside of town," I said. "Can I get coffee for two?"

"Cream and sugar?" she asked.

"Milk for me," I said, because in America's Dairyland, cream is processed and packaged and brought from somewhere else, for some unknown reason. Milk is fresh and local. "I don't know if she wants cream or sugar, so you can bring those, too."

A low buzz came through the window and two front-loaders went by on Main Street. Their buckets were raised, and the guys driving didn't look like a road crew. Maybe they were a digging crew. Maybe they were a demolition crew. They moved as fast as the rest of the traffic until they disappeared. The waitress brought a carafe of coffee and two mugs.

A couple of minutes past noon, Sarah bounced past my window and through the door. She saw me and slid in across. "You made it," she said.

"You thought I wouldn't?"

She paused and decided to be honest. "I wasn't sure what to expect."

"You can expect me to show up when you're buying," I said. "What's good here?"

She smiled and said, "Fish. Local is walleye and lake perch, but there's cod, pollack, mahi mahi and . . . salmon, too."

I looked at her instead of the menu and said, "Walleye sounds good."

"You'll want it battered," she said.

"Battered sounds good," I said.

That's when the guy in the leather jacket came up the sidewalk. A few seconds later, he was inside the diner.

It was the first leather jacket I'd seen that day, and his jeans were out of the ordinary, too. They were dark blue, almost black. And neat and new. Different from the old, clean jeans worn by the old timers. Different from the dirty jeans worn by the younger guys. Different from everybody.

He scanned the room, a half-second on each face, and I saw he was different in another way: He was aware.

He was comparing each face to the database in his head.

Which was an activity I recognized, because I had done the same thing when I walked into the diner.

And he was doing another thing I had done: He was filing away faces. So that the faces he saw now could be compared to other faces later. He was growing his database of faces under the filename of Jake's hometown.

But he wasn't only looking at faces. He was looking at coats for bulges. He was looking for the slight shift in weight that showed something hidden. He was looking for things beneath the surface. He was looking for weapons. Just like I had done.

A CIA support officer once told me that she usually didn't need a description to pick up CIA officers in airports. She didn't need to know their hair color or the clothes they were wearing. She didn't need to know whether they were carrying a backpack or a roller bag. She just needed to know what time they would show up, and she could pick them out. She could pick them out, she told me, because CIA officers were always more aware than everyone else.

Not that he was a CIA officer. Or even an ex-CIA officer like me.

There are lots of other professions that train people to be aware. He could be a cop. Or an ex-cop. Or a criminal. Or an assassin.

Whatever he was, he was aware.

Which was a problem for me. Because aware people don't just look for faces, shifts of weight, and bulges that could be weapons. They also look for other people who are aware.

An aware person looks for who else is collecting data and building a database of faces and analyzing threats.

Which means there's another skill you need

to develop when you're aware: How to turn it off.

Before the leather-coated guy got to my face, I turned off my awareness.

I turned off the questions in my head. I turned off the questions about where the guy was from. About what he was doing here, when he obviously wasn't from here.

The best way to turn off awareness is to focus on something right in front of you and ignore everything else.

I focused on Sarah. Which is what a mostly average guy like me should be doing anyway with a pretty girl in front of him. I asked her, "Do you drink coffee? Or tea?"

"Just water," she said.

"Are you sure?" I asked. "You're buying."

She smiled. "You keep reminding me."

"I'm wondering why you wanted to buy me lunch," I said.

"Because I expect you to buy next time," she said. "Reciprocity has to start on one side or the other, so I started it."

"Does that mean I'm buying you lunch or dinner next time?" I asked.

She shrugged. "How long are you in town?"

It depended on the guy who had walked in and how many others he brought with him, but I didn't say that. Instead I said, "A few days, probably."

"What is it you do, exactly?"

"I'm a consultant," I said.

"What does that mean?" she asked.

"I help people collect data and analyze it, so they make good decisions."

"People pay for that?" she asked.

"Most of the time," I said. "It depends on the decision they need to make. And the data they need collected. And the questions they need answered"

As I was talking to her, I was thinking about the decisions I was about to make.

And the questions I needed to answer:

1. Was the leather-coated guy in town for me?

2. If so, was it just him or were there more?

3. If so, what were his capabilities?

Chapter 10

I had never fought a woman before.

Not even in training.

Maybe it's a vestige of the twentieth century male-only spy world, but my trainers never had me spar with a woman. It was an oversight on their part. After all, the point of training is to be sure you don't do something for the first time in the field. Because the first time you do anything new, chances are you'll get it wrong. Including fighting a woman.

With the gun on the floor of the Abu Dhabi hotel room and a woman coming at me, I had to figure out how to fight a woman for the first time.

My first action was to do nothing at all. Societal training or parental influence or an old sense of chivalry told me not to hit a woman. And she was definitely a woman. So I did nothing.

Then she took a step toward me and was close enough to do some damage with a jab. Societal training or parental influence or an old sense of chivalry told me that I shouldn't hit a woman, but I also didn't need to take a beating from a woman if she came at me. So my second action was to raise my hands in defense.

She was about my height, which is tall for a woman, since I'm mostly average for a man. Her brown eyes were at eye level and half-focused in a way to let her see movement in a wider sphere. Her dark hair was pulled back. Exposed on her left cheek were three scars. They were each a half inch long, rising from her jawline. That's where I'd try to hit her, if she was a man.

But she wasn't a man, so my third action was to ask a question. "Who are you?"

She didn't answer.

Instead she flashed her right hand at my face and flicked her wrist. I'm quicker than average, but so was she.

I didn't react in time. Her palm connected with my chin and pushed my head backward.

I stumbled back two steps and landed on the bed.

There was a lamp and a glass water bottle I could have used for weapons, but societal training or parental influence or an old sense of chivalry told me it wasn't fair to pick them up. Because I wouldn't use them as weapons. And threatening to use weapons without intending to use weapons is a kind of lie. A lie is a terrible way to start a relationship with a woman. So I left everything where it was.

Instead, I stood up and said, "Okay, you're not here to kill me or you would have left when you lost your weapon. So you're here to ask questions, right? You want to know who I am? Go ahead. Ask the questions."

Instead, she reached down and pulled a Ruger 9mm from her ankle holster and aimed it at me.

In that moment, I learned another thing about fighting a woman: They usually have a backup weapon. Maybe, two backup weapons. If a man loses his weapon, his backup is usually his fists. If a woman loses her weapon, her fists probably won't win. Her fists or hands are used to push back the guy so she can pull her backup weapon.

I waited, and she didn't shoot me, which meant she probably wasn't going to shoot me at all.

Instead, she asked, "Who are you?"

Her accent was flat. No high tones like French. No deep tones like German or Arabic. Flat, like she was from the American Midwest. Like me.

"Zach Middleton," I said. "How can I help you?"

"How old is your passport, Zach?" She fished

around in my bag on the table and found it. "Two months old. And this is your first passport stamp? You don't seem like a guy who would have just one passport stamp."

I could have said I lost my old one. Or I could have said my old one expired and this one just arrived. Or I could have said it was my first passport. But I don't like to delay the inevitable. And I was trying not to start the relationship with a lie.

So I asked, "Why did your boss send a woman, not a man? Does that mean he doesn't want to do this by force? No offense."

Her eyebrows went up. "My boss? Who is my boss?"

Her teeth weren't orthodontically perfect the way an American's would be. They were straight in the front, but the canines on both sides went a little forward.

Then she blinked, and her right contact slipped. There was green behind a brown contact.

She wasn't exactly American, but she could pass for one. And she had a second weapon ready in case she lost the first one. Plus, she had no comms in her ear, which meant she was trusted to act alone.

I had a hypothesis about her boss, so I tested it. "Your boss is some guy who doesn't appreciate what you do. He's always putting the guys on the team ahead of you, especially when you're operating in the Middle East." There was a little flicker on her face, so I kept going. "Today, you got the worst job on the surveillance team: setting up in the mall. You were probably there for an hour before I got there, but that meant you were the one who saw me, so you made the case to your boss to send you to my door. You told him you were the only one who could get a positive ID and be sure the guy in the hotel room was the same guy in the mall."

While I was talking, I was thinking through who she could be with. There are only few intelligence agencies besides the CIA who send out women alone, and my boss should have deconflicted to be sure no other CIA people were here. Plus, there are only a few agencies that care about developing nuclear bombmakers in the Middle East. And there are fewer still who train their people to use palm strikes to the chin.

Put it all together, and it meant she was probably Mossad. Or maybe Shin Bet. Or possibly some Israeli military unit I hadn't heard of. Either way, she was Israeli.

"Who are you?" she asked again, with a different meaning.

She really didn't know. In fact, I could be another Israeli.

Israeli spies have the same problems every spy organization has: With compartmentalization and multiple organizations, sometimes people from the same government don't know that they're both working on the same guy. And the bombmaker

I was supposed to meet was a hot prospect, which meant lots of scouts.

Question #1 for her was if I was Israeli. She couldn't kill me until she knew the answer.

I knew a few words of Hebrew. Enough to say I'm not Israeli. So I said it. "ישראלי לא אני" Which sounded like "Ani Lo Isry-ali."

It was also a test to see if she really was Israeli.

She was, because she spoke back to me in Hebrew that I didn't understand.

In English, I said, "I'm American – CIA. How about you put the gun down and tell me your name?"

She thought for a moment, then lowered her gun and thought some more. She couldn't give me the alias she was using, because I could tie it back to her movements later. And she couldn't give me her real name. Which meant she could either ignore my question or give me a third name.

"What's your name?" I asked again.

"Esther," she decided.

Standing there, she didn't have a random name generator like a baseball roster. She didn't have an outside data source. Which meant it was probably her grandmother's name or maybe the name of a friend who had died. A name she would be proud to bear. A name of honor or homage. A name connected to her.

"Hi Esther," I said. "I'm not here to get in your way. It'd be great if you didn't get in my way. Are you going to kill the nuclear bombmaker?"

Esther looked at me and went through her three options:

1. Be honest, if an ally.
2. Lie, if an enemy.
3. Don't answer, if you're not sure.

She made her decision and laughed.

She said, "He's not a nuclear bombmaker."

Chapter 11

I was still ignoring the leather-coated guy as I finished my battered walleye at the diner in Wisconsin. Then, the waitress brought the guy his plate. I acted like I was following the waitress with my eyes, rather than looking at him.

The leather-coated guy took his plate from the waitress, which gave me a chance to look at his ankles.

His right ankle was angled away from me, but his socks got thicker above the ankle bone. If he had an ankle holster and weapon in it, that's what it would look like from my side. On the other side of his ankle would be more of the holster and all of the gun. If he was a cop, it was probably a Smith & Wesson J-frame like the 360 or the 360 PD. Lightweight with .357 magnum rounds.

If he was in town for me, we'd meet. When we met, I'd need to clear his ankle to be sure the .357 magnum rounds didn't head in my direction.

I turned back to Sarah before the leather-coated guy caught my awareness and looked back at me.

"Do you like the waitress?" she asked.

Sarah was aware. At least, she was aware of what I was watching. Especially, if I was watching another women.

I said, "The hamburger she gave that guy looks good. Maybe I'll get one next time."

The guy would take at least fifteen minutes to eat his burger and pay his check. To be set up to surveil the leather-coated guy when he left the diner, I needed to be in place at least five minutes before he finished his burger. Which meant it was time to leave Sarah.

But first, Sarah said, "Don't you want to know

why I clean houses?"

"Not for the money?" I asked.

"It's not just for the money," she answered. "I could make more in a sit-down office job or selling something."

"Okay," I said. "Why are you cleaning houses?"

"Because each house is a fun little investigation," she said. "I like to ask myself questions as I clean. Questions like, 'Why is that chair facing away from the window? Why are the floor lights missing from this room?' There are new questions every week. Or every two weeks, in the case of your house."

"What do you find out?" I asked.

"I can tell when there's a death in the family or someone has a grandchild born or if their money is about to run out," Sarah said. "Your house is strange. None of the personal items are touched. Which is what I see when there's a death in the family. The person's personal things don't get touched. They become like a shrine."

Which explained why Sarah wanted to have lunch and offered to pay for it: She had questions.

It was true I hadn't touched many of Jake's things since he'd died. I'd left his toothbrush where it was. His towel still hung on the rack. His bedroom was the way it was. I slept in the second bedroom.

But I hadn't left Jake's things that way to be a shrine. I'd left them because I didn't intend on being Jake Beamer forever, and I didn't want to make his house mine.

I wondered if it was bad luck that I'd found an inquisitive house cleaner or if most house cleaners were like her.

"I'm still here," I said. "Not dead yet."

She smiled. "I know. But you're different from others around here. Maybe it's because you travel. Your life is elsewhere. So you don't know how to make a home."

I wasn't sure if she was talking about me or

Jake at that point, so I said, "I'm here for a few more days, at least. When I'm done with my project, I'll take you to lunch or dinner and you can investigate me some more."

"When, exactly?" she asked.

"The project will probably last a few days, but it doesn't have a defined deadline," I said. "I'll call you. What's your number?"

She gave it to me. Then, she paid the waitress with the money I'd overpaid her. We said good-bye, and she went to the restroom while I left.

Outside the diner, I turned the corner and walked past a little hardware store, a paint store and a tax accountant's office. At the end of the block, I went right and retrieved Jake's car. Since I had time, I turned left on the street behind Main Street and back across Main Street a few blocks down. Another left and another left, and I was a few yards from Main Street one block up from the diner. I reversed into a spot on the far side of the street in front of a store advertising antiques. From there, I could see the diner's front door.

After seven minutes, the guy in the leather coat came out with a to-go cup of coffee. He stood in the doorway for a few seconds and scanned the area. His eyes passed over my car and back to the buildings in front of him. He was comparing what he saw to what he'd seen. And he was adding to the database in his head.

Just like I would have done.

He turned left, which was the opposite direction from which he'd come. Which means he had taken the long way around to get to the diner.

Just like I would have done.

He got in a car parked on Main Street. It was pointed toward me, so he waited for a gap in traffic and did a U-turn in the middle of the street.

I didn't follow him, because following him wouldn't give me any more data.

If he was in town for me, I'd see him on the

cameras at the entrance to Jake's street.

If he wasn't in town for me, I'd never see him again.

Ten minutes passed. Then, fifteen.

Then, I got an alert on my phone that a car had passed one of the cameras at the entrance to Jake's street.

Chapter 12

It's no accident Israeli and American intelligence services get along. Two nations run by recent foreigners. Both lands full of people who started somewhere else.

Which also helps you spy.

When Russians send out spies, they look Russian. When Cubans send out spies, they look Cuban. When Nigerians send out spies, if they ever do, they look Nigerian.

When Americans and Israelis send out spies, they don't necessarily look American or Israeli. They might look Russian. Or Cuban. Or Nigerian.

Which is an advantage.

An advantage most nations don't have.

Including the nation the nuclear bombmaker

came from.

"He's not a nuclear bombmaker," said Esther again. "He's an intel officer."

I went back over what I knew about the guy. All the background the targeting officer at headquarters had given me. And what I'd seen in the mall. "He doesn't look like an intel officer," I said.

"Neither do you," said Esther.

I nodded. "Right, but he doesn't look like an intel officer from any country in the Middle East. They're not like us, as you know. They're more straightforward. They're not trying to pretend to be anybody else. They're not trying to be double agents."

Esther shrugged. "I was told he's an intel officer."

Which I thought had a 50/50 chance of being true. The Israeli intel could be wrong. Or Esther could be lying to me. So I asked a follow-up question, because it's always easier to see if someone is lying when they're answering a question they didn't expect.

"Did they turn a nuclear bombmaker into an intel officer? Or did they teach an intel officer about nuclear bombmaking?"

"I don't know," she said.

Which meant she wasn't trying to lie. If she was trying to lie, she would have made something up.

She was probably repeating what she'd been told. The person who told her could have been lying, but it's less likely someone would lie to someone on their own side. So I adjusted the probability to 80 percent that the bombmaker was an intel officer. Which meant there was a 20 percent chance he wasn't.

Either way, it didn't matter. Because it would take me only three questions to find out what he was when I met him.

Now, it was time for a more difficult question for Esther. I asked her, "Are you going to kill him?"

I saw her go through the three options of

honesty, lying and deflection again.

Esther decided to be honest. "I don't know." Or she wasn't really answering, which meant she still wasn't sure about me.

I assumed the best. "If you don't know, that means a decision hasn't been made. You guys haven't decided because you're waiting on something else. Were you waiting to see who he would meet? If so, you know it's me. Now, you know there's no immediate risk. So you can take a breath."

She nodded. "What are you going to do?"

"I'm going to go meet him," I said. "I was just about to send him an email."

She looked at me incredulously. "Wait a minute. You still want to meet him?"

"He's not going to kill me the first time I meet him," I said. "If he's an intel officer, he's going to need to verify I'm CIA before he kills me, right? And if he's a nuclear bombmaker, he won't try to kill me. Either way, he's not going to kill me the first time he meets me. Do you think he's going to kill me the first time he meets me?"

She considered everything. "Probably not."

"Probably not," I agreed.

"But we should talk to my boss," she said.

"Why?" I asked. "He's going to ask me a bunch of questions I can't answer."

"Because the plan was to kill this guy after we found out who you were. If you go meet him, you'll get caught in the middle."

Which was different from what she had said just a minute before.

I considered everything. "Okay. I'll meet your boss."

"Good," she said. "Turn around."

"Turn around?" I repeated. "Why?"

"I need to change," she said.

I turned around and faced the window. In the reflection, I saw a flash of white underwear as she pulled off the maid's uniform. She pulled a bag from the trash side of the maid's carrel and took out black western pants. She pulled them up over her ankle holster and over her hips. A dark blue shirt went over her head. The bottom of the shirt fell loosely at her waist.

"You can turn back around," she said. She pulled out her ponytail, and long brown hair fell to her shoulders. She turned to the mirror above the desk and took out the brown contacts.

Esther took a deep breath and faced me. Everything about her was different. Her clothes and her demeanor. And her eyes were green.

It was a bigger change than a name change.

She was unconnected to the maid who knocked on the door.

"Let's go see my boss," she said.

"First, a couple of questions," I said.

She nodded.

"Where were you in the mall?" I asked.

"On the far side on the third floor."

I went through my memories. "In a blue hijab?"

She nodded.

"How did you know to set up there in advance?" I asked. I knew the answer, because it was the only answer, but I wanted to give her one more chance to decide whether to lie to me or tell me the truth.

"We hacked his emails," she said.

I nodded. "Okay. Let's go see your boss."

Chapter 13

The guy in the leather coat did what I would have done: He drove past Jake's house, circled back at the end of the road and paused at the chokepoint.

I watched it happen in a series of still photos and short videos. First, one of the hunting cameras sent me a picture taken at the entrance, then I got a 1.5 second video when he passed Jake's house. Then another one second video on the way back five minutes later. And another still photo twenty seconds after that.

Then, he left, and I had the answer to Question 1: He was there for me.

But I didn't have the answer to Question 2: Was he alone or were there others? Were there more coming? Or was it just him?

The question was partially answered thirty-five minutes later when the hunting camera sent me another picture. It was a picture of the guy parked, nose out, in the same spot I had used when I set up the hunting camera.

He didn't choose a spot where he could stay at a distance. Instead, it was a spot chosen so he could follow me, as soon as he saw me. It wasn't a spot where he would stay after I passed and call others to get on my tail. It was a spot where he could do all the work himself.

Which meant he was probably on his own. The answer to Question 2: Probably alone.

To be sure, I decided to wait. I decided to wait until it would be time to be relieved from his surveillance post, if he was going to be relieved from his surveillance post.

After two hours, nobody else had showed up. He got out and relieved himself in the woods behind his car. Just before the four-hour mark, he did it again.

Which meant he probably wasn't expecting anyone else soon.

More and more likely: He was alone.

It was after the daylight savings time change and some weeks before the solstice, so the next hour was the sun setting above the trees. I let him settle back into the semi-conscious state I knew from doing surveillance myself.

When you sit for a long time, your heart rate goes down. Your blood flow slows.

When I did surveillance, I used breathing to settle in. One long inhale on a five second count and slow exhales. It took ten or so until my body settled into the car seat or the park bench or the restaurant booth. Until the blood was flowing steady and even through my body. Until my mind ebbed and the only thing to think about was what I was watching for.

I didn't know if the leather-coated guy used breathing, but he'd need to find some way to stay alert. Maybe he would use energy drinks. Maybe a nootropic. Maybe a harder drug. Or maybe he used a podcast or a book on tape. Whatever it was, it wouldn't keep him fully alert. He'd settle into a low-conscious state after a couple of hours.

That's what I waited for.

When he was thirty minutes into his sixth hour, I started toward him.

I parked in a gas station lot three-quarters of a mile away and started jogging along the road toward the entrance to Jake's street.

Six hundred yards from the entrance I turned into the woods. I ran parallel for seventy-five yards, then turned toward it.

Three hundred yards from the entrance, headlights played into the woods, and I slowed down.

Two hundred yards from the entrance, I got an alert on my phone. I bent down behind a tree and opened the message.

There was a car in the photo. A car with the squiggly lines printed on the back window: SGB.

The car was Sarah's.

I got another alert, and a video showed Sarah pulling into Jake's driveway.

The next alert on my phone was a picture of the leather-coated guy's car in a new position. His car was aimed toward Jake's house.

A few seconds later, a video on my phone showed him pulling into the driveway behind Sarah.

I ran.

Chapter 14

Soviet Premier Nikita Khrushchev had a son named Sergei. Sergei Khrushchev was a scientist who moved to the United States after the Berlin Wall fell. After he had lived in America for a while, somebody asked Sergei to compare the people in his homeland to Americans.

Sergei said the difference was that the Soviet people grew up in a jungle. Americans, Sergei said, were "a tiger that grew up in the zoo and then was sent into the jungle."

It's a little insulting to us Americans, but when I met Esther's boss, that quote crossed my mind. When I met him, it felt like I was meeting a tiger who grew up in the jungle.

Esther's boss didn't look like a Russian. Or a

Cuban. Or a Nigerian. He looked like what you'd expect an Israeli to look like. But bigger. And more catlike. Which is probably what made me think of Sergei Khrushchev's statement.

He paced back and forth but kept his eyes on me. Like he was choosing the best angle of attack.

"CIA," he said. "I should have known."

I smiled. "Nice to meet you. Are you going to get in the way of me meeting this guy?"

"Where are you from?" he asked. "What part of America?"

"The middle part," I answered. "Are you going to get in the way?"

He shrugged. "Maybe."

I shrugged and turned to go. "Okay. Let me know when you've made a decision."

A big paw landed on my shoulder. "Just a minute. You don't care? You don't care which one we do?"

I shook off his paw and turned toward him.

"Not really. I don't have much time invested. And now that you guys are involved, everything is more complicated, so I'm happy to walk away. But if you guys stay out of the way, I'll go through with the meeting and see if I can recruit him."

Esther's boss laughed. "It's that simple?"

I shrugged. "Pretty much. Am I missing something?"

He shook his head. "When I talk to the CIA, it's usually more complicated."

"That's because you talk to CIA station chiefs or office people or technical people. Their job is more complicated than mine. My job is to recruit spies and collect intelligence. My job is simple."

Esther's boss turned to Esther. "Can you believe this guy?"

"Listen," I said. "I'm your only chance to make a non-threatening approach. You hacked his emails, but you can't send him an email that he'll trust. Only I can do that. Only I can tell him where to go and be confident he'll show up."

Esther's boss frowned at Esther, so I interjected. "I knew you hacked his emails because you were set up in the mall before I got there. Which means you knew where he was going and where he'd be. By reading his emails."

Esther chose a side and said, "Let him meet the guy. We can see what happens." Which made me glad I hadn't started our relationship with a lie.

Esther's boss paused for a moment, then laughed again. "All right. All right. Let's do it. You meet with the guy, but we'll be there, in case something happens."

It seemed too easy, so I asked, "And then what? What happens after I meet him?"

Esther's boss said, "If you can recruit him, we run him jointly."

Which was possible. But running a source jointly with the Israelis was not up to me. It would be decided by the station chiefs, office people and technical people. People with more complicated jobs. I just needed to know one thing, so I'd know if my time would be wasted.

"You won't kill him?" I asked.

Esther's boss shook his head. "Not right away."

I went back to my hotel and sat down where I was when Esther knocked on the door. I opened the VPN and got ready to send the email to the nuclear bombmaker.

Before I sent it, I stopped and imagined the worst case. Could this be some convoluted double-agent operation? Could Esther be actually working for some other intel service? Maybe from the same country as the nuclear bombmaker?

No. The surveillance through the mall was real. Esther with the guns was real. It hadn't been smooth, and Esther had been just a little bit off, which is normal when things are real. Plus, her ethnicity was wrong, and she responded to the Hebrew I spoke. And her boss was a real Israeli.

I sent an email apologizing to the nuclear bombmaker for missing the meeting. My flight had been delayed, I said.

Could he meet the next day at the same place?

Twenty-three minutes later, he replied that he could.

Chapter 15

In the Wisconsin woods, it was a race.

The leather-coated guy was in a car.

I was on foot.

He won by a lot.

By the time I was in view of Jake's house, the leather-coated guy was standing in front of his car. In the headlights, he was talking to Sarah.

Sarah didn't seem alarmed. Or worried. Or bothered in any way. She stood there, listening to what the leather-coated guy was telling her.

I didn't know what he was saying, but it was probably something about me.

I popped out my phone and called Sarah's number from behind a tree.

She pulled the vibrating phone out of her pocket and said, "Hi Jake. I stopped by to pick up a cleaning bottle I left this morning." She turned toward the house. "Are you home?"

I said, "Listen to me and do exactly what I say, okay? Say 'okay.'"

"Okay," she said.

"Don't look at the guy who pulled into the driveway behind you, but he's there for me and he's dangerous, I think."

"You think?" she said and stayed facing the house.

"Did he say something about being an old buddy from the military? Did he give you a reason to tell him where I am and keep it a surprise?"

"Yes," she said.

"Okay," I said. "Can you think of a bar where a lot of guys will have guns? If so, say the name and meet me there. Tell the guy to meet me there, too."

"Oswald's?" she asked with a hard edge.

"Okay," I said. "Oswald's. Tell him I said I'm at Oswald's and you're going to meet me there."

"Okay," she said.

"Okay," I said. "Take the slow way there so I can get there in time. Don't worry. Everything will be all right."

"I know," she said. "Bye."

I stayed in the woods.

After a short discussion with Sarah, the leather-coated guy reversed his car out of Jake's driveway and waited for Sarah to do the same. Their headlights played across the tree I stood behind, then pointed toward the entrance. I waited until their brake lights were out of sight, then sprinted back again through the dark pines.

Thirteen minutes later, I was at my parked car. I pulled out my phone, found out how to get to Oswald's and sped toward it.

By the time I got there, everything was over.

Chapter 16

I wasn't an expert on nuclear bombmaking, but I didn't need to be.

To find out if the nuclear bombmaker in Abu Dhabi was really a nuclear bombmaker, it wasn't necessary to be an expert. All I had to do was ask the right questions. If I did it right, it would take only three questions.

Whether it's nuclear bombmaking or 18th century art or a made-up identity, if someone doesn't know the subject well, it's hard for them to answer three questions deep.

If they're prepared, they can answer the first question, no problem. If they're well-prepared, they can answer most of the second questions. But no matter how well-prepared someone is, it's hard to answer the third question, unless they're an expert.

Of the first-level questions, there might be ten that aren't facile or uninteresting. So the first question you ask is one of those ten. If it's 18th century art, you might ask them which artists were the real revolutionaries of their time. Or which artist is likely to be most valuable to collectors in the next decade. Or which artist had the most impact on the 19th century. Those are easy questions to answer, if you're prepared to answer questions about 18th century art.

But after the first question, the next is more difficult. If the first question was about the artist with the impact on the 19th century, then there are at least ten follow-up questions you could ask about specific works or influences or successors to that artist.

At that point, you're one hundred questions deep. Because there were ten top-level questions plus ten second-level questions on each one. That's one hundred potential questions you could ask. Which someone who is well-prepared might be ready for.

Then comes the third level. Ten potential follow-up questions on each one of those one hundred questions, and you're at a thousand possible questions.

If the guy isn't an expert, he definitely won't be able to answer a thousand questions.

Which means, if the guy wants to pretend he's an expert, he's going to get creative on the third question. He's going to start making things up. He's going to lie. Which is what you want.

Because the best way to find out if someone is a liar is to give them a chance to lie.

Since Esther and her boss didn't think this guy was a real nuclear bombmaker, I started with a general question: "What are you most excited about in your field?"

He answered with a five-minute explanation of the various methods of isotope separation.

I didn't know a lot about isotope separation,

but I knew enough to ask him about which method he thought had the most promise.

He answered with another five-minute explanation of his favorite method. He was experimenting with several variations in order to develop more expertise.

By that time, he had thrown out a lot of jargon. And acronyms. And when I asked for what each acronym and jargon meant, he explained each. After all of that, I was ninety-five percent sure he was a real expert.

But I wanted to be a hundred percent sure, so I asked a third question: "What are most marketable technologies you think will come from this method of isotope separation?"

He looked at me blankly. "I'm sorry," he said. "What do you mean?"

"I mean, do you think there are any potential uses for your techniques and technology that can make us a lot of money?"

He laughed and shrugged. "I don't know. I'm just an engineer."

Which was a good answer. I'd given him a chance to lie or make things up, and he didn't take it.

It looked like Esther was wrong.

He wasn't an intel officer, everything told me.

He was an expert. And he didn't take the opportunity to lie, like an intelligence officer would have.

But more than that, he wasn't aware.

He wasn't watching the environment. He wasn't placing people and tracking people and comparing people to pictures in his head. He wasn't like the bearded guy at the Dubai airport. He wasn't aware of what was happening around us.

When you're a spy, threats are less likely to come from the guy across the table than from outside. Maybe you missed that you were under surveillance, and the surveillance team is closing in. Maybe the guy you're meeting was under surveillance. Or maybe, it's a random street criminal who sees you as a target of opportunity.

Whatever the source of the threat, threats are more likely to come from someone other than the guy at the table with you.

Spies know that. Which is why spies always keep an eye on the environment.

This guy wasn't keeping an eye on the environment. Which meant he was unlikely to be a spy.

But I was.

I was watching the environment as the nuclear bombmaker was telling me about isotope separation techniques and his experiments.

Which is why I saw the bearded man from the airport before anyone else did.

Chapter 17

When I pushed through the door of Oswald's in Wisconsin, there were four large men standing around Sarah. The largest one had a gun in his hand.

Sarah nodded at me and said, "That's Jake."

The gun was loose in the largest guy's hand and wasn't pointed at me. I said, "Hi guys. What's going on?"

"Good question," said the largest one. "Why did a guy with a gun come in here with Sarah?"

I turned back toward the door. "Where did he go?"

Two of the large men stepped between me and the door, and the largest one spoke again for the group. "He's gone. What's going on?"

I let my mind become aware. I looked at

each of the four guys and captured their micromovements. I looked for which ones were righties and which ones were lefties. I analyzed it all and built a plan for winning a fight. I would start with the guy who hadn't spoken and hadn't moved. Then, the two by the door.

The largest one with the gun would be last, unless I got lucky with angles and pushed the second or third guy into him.

Sarah saw me tense up and took a step toward me. "Jake, relax. These are my brothers: Ed, Joey, Jimmy and Ryan. Well, Ryan's a cousin, but he's like a brother." Ed was the largest one. Joey and Jimmy were the ones by the door. Ryan was the one I was going to attack first.

Ed put the gun in his waist belt and said, "Sarah, go sit at the bar. We'll send him over in a minute."

She started to protest, but Ed said, "Go." She backed out of the circle. Ed, Joey, Jimmy and Ryan surrounded me again.

Ed said, "What kind of trouble are you into?"

Since they were allies, I decided to be honest. "I don't know. I'm trying to find out."

"Who was that guy?"

"I'm trying to find that out, too. Did you check his ankle for a holster?"

Joey and Jimmy looked at each other and said, "No."

I said, "What you took from him is a Glock 23, which makes it likely he's a cop. If he had an ankle holster, too and a PD model in it, that would confirm it. But he's not a cop from around here, so you don't need to worry about him doing anything to you. He's probably freelancing. But that's just a hypothesis. I would have known for sure if you hadn't let him go."

Ed said, "Who are you exactly?"

Even though they were allies, that was the one question I had to answer with a lie. "Jake Beamer," I said.

"What's your experience with this kind of thing?" asked Ed.

I didn't want to give them Jake's biography and I didn't want to give them mine, but I didn't want to lie any more than I had to. So I said, "Government work. Overseas."

At that, there was a micromovement from all four. They leaned back.

Ed asked, "How do we know you're the good guy in all this?"

"I didn't come in here chasing your sister with a gun," I said.

Ed nodded. Jimmy and Joey looked at each other and nodded. Ryan stayed where he was and didn't move.

"Do you need any help?" asked Ed.

I shook my head. "I usually work alone. Did the guy say anything before he left?" I asked.

"No," said Ed. "He just looked around and left."

The leather-coated guy and I had the same goal: A confrontation. He was looking for me, and I was looking for him. We were like two armies circling, trying to find a battlefield. We both wanted the fight. The question was where and when.

For where and when, the leather-coated guy had two options:

1. Go back to the entrance to Jake's street and wait for me; or

2. Wait up the street for me to drive away from Oswald's.

If he wanted the fight sooner, he'd take Option #2. And Option #2 got his eyes on me sooner, too.

If he took Option #2, he wasn't far.

If he took Option #2, he was waiting outside.

If he took Option #2, I could take some time before I left. There was no hurry.

I turned back to Ed and said, "Can you keep Sarah here for a couple of hours? I think this will be over soon."

"You're not going to tell us what this is all about?" asked Ed.

"Like I said: I'm trying to figure it out," I said.

"Okay, but it's hard to keep Sarah anywhere she doesn't want to be," said Ed. "I'll let you tell her."

At the bar, Sarah already had a beer in front of her and one next to her for me. I sat down and said, "Sorry you got in the middle."

"Is this guy the 'consulting project' you were working on?" she asked.

"He's part of it," I said.

"Who is your client?" she asked.

"He's dead," I said.

"And you're still working for him?"

"That's right. If you don't mind staying here for a few hours, I'll finish it up."

"Stay here why?" she asked.

"So I don't have to worry about you," I answered.

"Okay. Still on for lunch or dinner in a few days?"

"Yes," I said. "I'll give you a call."

"All right," she said.

I dropped cash on the bar and went out into the dirty parking lot to look for the leather-coated guy.

Chapter 18

In the Abu Dhabi mall, Sergei Khrushchev's statement came to mind again. As the Israelis and the bearded man's security moved around each other, they looked like big cats circling.

Like in the jungle, for what happened next, there would be no rules made by any legal authority or common morality or mutual agreement. Everything would be decided by force.

When it comes down to force, risks are high, which means math becomes important. Especially, the math of strength and probability.

Each side spent the first five seconds identifying who and how many were on the other side. In those seconds, each Israeli picked out one of the bearded man's men and stepped between him and me. I counted them as even in numbers. Except I couldn't see Esther, which meant the Israelis outnumbered them by one. Unless the bearded men had people hidden, too.

A mother with two children felt the change in the air. She looked up and a half-second later was pulling her children out of their seats and into their stroller. One of them cried, but the mother didn't slow down. By the time both sides were in position, she was pushing the stroller away.

Everyone else in the mall was oblivious. Five people in line at the ice cream store and seven people walking past a clothes boutique and two couples laughing by the window didn't notice the change. The ice cream store people were looking at the list of flavors and at the bins under glass. The seven people walking by kept on walking. The two couples by the window kept laughing.

They didn't notice that the mall had become a jungle.

Someone would attack first. Just like how the first guy to throw a punch in a fight usually wins, the first guy to pull out his gun in a gunfight usually wins.

But these guys were experienced. They knew that pulling a gun in a mall would mean their careers were over. The cameras would catch them, and they'd never be able to operate anywhere again, if they survived. Because they might not survive. The other side had guns, too. Pulling out their guns first meant the probability of surviving the next two minutes was higher, but so was the probability of a long-term loss.

One guy approached my table. Another stepped in between. On one side, I couldn't tell which was which. I didn't know which one to root for.

The bombmaker was oblivious. Definitely not an intel officer. He was still telling me about isotope separation, and I wasn't listening.

I was thinking about my options.

The bearded man's men didn't know me. They didn't know who I was or why I was sitting with the bombmaker. If I got up and walked away, they'd probably let me go. They were there for the bombmaker. They weren't there for me.

I could walk away.

But then the bombmaker would be fought over. The way jungle cats fight over prey. Which usually doesn't turn out well for the prey.

The Israelis would kill him before they'd let the bearded man's men get him. And who knows what the bearded man would do with the bombmaker if he got him.

Which would mean I'd never recruit this guy as a source. Which would mean I wasted time on this trip and all the preparation for it.

I hate wasting time.

I cut off whatever the bombmaker was

saying.

"Listen," I said, "Look at me."

But he was already looking at me, so he was confused. "What?" he asked.

"I'm going to tell you something, and you're going to want to do the opposite. Don't do the opposite. Do exactly what I say, okay?"

The bombmaker shifted in his chair. "What do you mean?"

"This is going to be like engineering, where you follow the instructions of the guy who did it before you, okay? This is not a time for creativity. This is a time for following instructions, okay?"

That was when the bombmaker wanted to look around, so I stopped him. "Look at me. Eyes on me, for the next minute, okay?"

"Okay," he nodded.

"Something will happen, but you can't watch it," I said. "Your life is in danger, and the only way out is to do what I do. Don't look around. Look at me. If there's a bang, don't look at it.

Look at me. Keep your eyes on me. Whatever I do, you do, okay?"

The bombmaker looked at me, and the factors fell into place. He ran the equation and came up with the right answer. "You're a spy."

I nodded. "A spy on your side," I said. "There are guys here who aren't on your side and aren't on my side. But they don't like each other more than they care about you and me. Don't look around. When it comes time to move, you need to do what I do, but stay five steps behind me. Okay?"

While he was thinking about whether he was going to do what I did or not, the fire alarm went off.

On the far wall, I saw a woman in a blue hijab moving away from a pulled alarm.

Esther.

There were only four people still in line at the ice cream store. They turned around and looked up at the ceiling, where a speaker blared the alarm. The people by the boutique stopped and looked up, too. The couples by the window stopped laughing.

There was that strange delay in an emergency when people make a mental adjustment. When they ask themselves, "Is this real?" When they wonder, "Was it my imagination that just happened?" When they look around to see if others are experiencing the same thing. When they see others reacting to the same thing, the question changes to: "What do I do now?"

"Get up," I said to the bombmaker. "Follow me. Five steps behind."

Chapter 19

In Jake's car in Oswald's dirty parking lot, I sat for a minute and looked for where I would be, if I were the leather-coated guy.

If I wanted to watch the bar, there was a spot half-way hidden sixty yards toward town. On the road away from the town was another spot next to an abandoned building.

But the leather-coated guy didn't know if I would go toward town or away from town, so he'd need to set up in a place where he could see both ways.

I started the car. The headlights showed a long, low store advertising motor sports equipment across the street. Motorcycles for the summer, snowmobiles for the winter. Because it was almost winter, it was mostly snowmobiles in the windows. I pulled up an overhead map on my phone. Satellite view showed a large parking lot in the back. From there, someone could sit and watch cars leave the bar in either direction. They could sit there and stay concealed.

That's where I'd be.

I widened the satellite view on my phone and looked at radius of five miles. I picked out a long, straight road without any houses around it. It was several miles away. Away from town, too. Good for a battlefield.

I pulled out of the bar's parking lot and turned toward it.

Three seconds later, a car came out from behind the motor sports store and followed me.

A mile later, I took another turn, just to be sure he would follow me.

He did.

I turned on a side road, drove through overhanging trees and ended up on the road

I'd chosen. It was two lanes of asphalt crowned at the center double-stripe. A slight incline for runoff went to half-paved, half-gravel shoulders. Like the satellite view said, it was surrounded by empty fields.

The leather-coated guy thought it was a good field of battle, too, because he didn't waste any time.

His headlights got larger in my rear-view mirror, and I heard his straining engine as he got close. I didn't change speeds or move.

I wanted to see what he planned to do.

He pulled into the lane where there would be oncoming traffic, if there had been any. There wasn't any. The road was long and straight.

He put his front wheel in line with my rear wheel. Then he edged away from me onto the half-gravel, half paved shoulder. I knew what was coming.

I knew what was coming because I'd seen it in Abu Dhabi.

He was trying to get momentum.

When he came across, I accelerated.

I was a little slow, and his front bumper banged into my rear fender. But I had accelerated enough. Where he hit me was too far back for what he wanted to do, but it was enough to knock me a little bit sideways. My rear wheels skidded sideways. I steered away from the turn and went on to the other shoulder. Gravel shot up, but I got back on the road.

Then, he tried to do exactly the same thing again. Which wasn't smart, because this time I was ready.

He came up beside me. He went left on to the shoulder to get sideways momentum.

Then, he steered into me.

In that half-second while he was coming toward me, I hit the brakes.

When his car hit mine, we were side-to-side. Front tire to front tire. Rear wheel to rear wheel. There was a soft smack as the two cars locked together. Instead of doing what he wanted to do, he pushed me sideways.

At the same time, I steered away from him and pulled the handbrake. My rear tires lost traction and slid sideways into the back of his car. The rear of my car pushed his rear wheels off their grip. The front of his car pushed into the front of mine.

Side-to-side, we spun.

The center of the spin was to my left. Which meant centrifugal force pulled me to my right.

He had opposite forces pulling on him, which made it easier to reach for his weapon. He pulled out a Glock and aimed at me.

When you're shooting a weapon, you're trained to do it the same way every time. You're trained to grip, aim and squeeze the same way every time. So it becomes part of your muscle memory. So it becomes automatic. So you do the same thing every time. Which is great, until doing the same thing doesn't get the same result. Until some other force intervenes.

Now, that force was centrifugal force.

When he gripped, aimed and squeezed his weapon, the centrifugal force pulled his arm up and sideways.

The muzzle flashed, and the bullet went through the ceiling of his car.

He pulled his arm back toward me to adjust, but the forces were pulling his arm in three dimensions. He overcompensated on one dimension but didn't adjust for the other two. A bullet sang by and smacked into the rear window of Jake's car.

The spin slowed. As soon as we were straight on the road, I lowered the handbrake and punched the gas. I sped out ahead and heard another bullet thunk into the rear glass.

But I didn't go too fast which meant I didn't go too far. To chase me, he was going to need to put down his weapon and get his car in gear, which was what I wanted.

When he started forward, I hit the brakes

and put Jake's car in reverse.

My seatbelt was on, but I hadn't seen if his was. For his sake and the sake of the questions I wanted to ask him, I hoped it was.

I hit him before he could get to a high speed. I wanted to stop him without hurting him too badly, if he wasn't wearing a seatbelt. But it had to be fast enough to trigger the airbag in his car, which it was.

On impact, my body's first movement was backward into the padded seat. His body's first movement was forward against his seatbelt and airbag.

If you've ever seen a crash in slow motion, you've seen that solids act like liquids.

At high speeds, the forces on solids look like waves. Crash test dummies convulse like break dancers. The energy moves part of their body up as another part goes down. Like the peak and trough of a wave.

It's also why nuclear programs employ experts in hydrodynamics, even though there are no liquids in a nuclear weapon. Because when things happen at high speeds, solids start to act like liquids. Energy moves in waves.

In a car crash, waves of energy take over. Your body buckles and convulses as the energy moves to your extremities. When the energy gets to your hands, it forces your fingers wide. It makes it impossible to hold a gun.

The waves of energy stopped.

My car and his car came to a stop on the side of the road.

Chapter 20

Sergei Khrushchev was wrong about the part about Americans growing up in a zoo. In a zoo, somebody gives you food for nothing. In a zoo, you have a separated environment. In a zoo, it's safe.

Growing up in the middle part of America was not safe. At least, not where I grew up.

Firearms were everywhere. The weather could lift your house away. Snakes and flash floods and near drownings happened every weekend.

Parents let you roam through it all. It wasn't their job to protect you. It was yours. Even from the bad people that drifted through. Which is why firearms were everywhere.

But maybe Sergei was talking about being

safe from predators. Maybe he was thinking that in a jungle you worry about what or who could attack you in the dark.

Like how the Russians worry about the Turks and the Ukrainians and the Chinese. Or like how the Turks worry about the Russians and the Syrians and the Cypriots. Or like how the Syrians worry about the Lebanese and the Israelis. You worry about them sneaking up on you in the dark. You worry about them finding your loved ones unprotected. Because nobody does worse things to other people than neighbors. Maybe that's the kind of jungle Sergei meant.

The nuclear bombmaker hadn't grown up in the jungle, either. He'd been separated from it by his education. He'd been in universities and laboratories and government institutes where the worst weapons are gossip.

Scientists like to think they're part of an international community. A community that spans borders and has a higher calling. They have rivalries within the disciplines and between universities and institutes and competition for funding, but they're still a community, they tell themselves. They're not part of the jungle. Their fights aren't settled by force.

The bombmaker hesitated when I told him to follow me. He was tempted to reason his way out of the situation in the Abu Dhabi mall. He wanted to collect more data. He wanted to spend more time analyzing it before he made a decision. But the only decision that was going to save his life was to follow me, so I said it again. More firmly, this time: "Follow me. Five steps behind. When I go, you go. When I stop, you stop!"

"Okay," he said. "Okay!"

With the fire alarm blaring, the Israelis and the bearded man's men stood still, hands over hidden guns.

You could see the calculations taking place.

Through all the games they were thinking

about and all the probabilities being guessed at and all the potential results, there were only two answers for the next action: Go or no go.

Nobody went.

Everyone stood still.

I walked up to the bearded man and said, "Hi there. You speak English?"

The bearded man flicked his eyes toward me, then to the bombmaker five steps behind me, then to the Israeli in front of him and back to me. He said, "Yes."

"This man behind me will follow me wherever I go. I'm going to walk with him outside and get in a car. You can follow, if you want. If you do, you can follow us to an area outside the city center where we can resolve this."

"We can resolve it here," said the bearded man.

I shook my head. "Not if you've thought this through. A gunfight in an Abu Dhabi mall won't make the locals happy, even if you're working with them. Soon, firefighters will be here and see the pulled fire alarm behind you. Then, they'll look at video footage and someone will leak that footage to the media. They'll have to act, even if you're working with them. Even if they already know you came in on the flight to Dubai last night."

At that, he looked at me again. "How did you know my flight?"

I shrugged. "It doesn't matter. What matters is that we leave before the firefighters arrive."

He shook his head. "I can't let him go."

"You're not letting him go," I said. "You're going with him someplace else."

He was a survivor of past battles. Which meant he knew when to fight and when not to fight.

He nodded.

I looked at Esther's boss. He nodded. "He can follow us."

The bearded man said, "My team will follow. I will go in your car." He spoke into an earpiece.

One of his men near me responded with, "Ay, Farhad." Which was Gulf Arabic for "Yes, Farhad." Which meant the bearded man's name, at least for here and now, was Farhad.

There were double-doors to a stairwell next to the elevator. An Israeli held one door, and one of Farhad's men held the other. We started toward it. I turned back to the bombmaker and nodded him forward.

The bombmaker didn't want to go forward. He wanted to walk away, which was understandable.

I pulled him aside and said, "Have you ever seen a nature documentary when two packs fight for prey?"

"What?" he asked. "What are you talking about?"

"You're the prey right now. I know you didn't expect to be prey when you woke up this morning. I know you've never thought of yourself as prey before. But that's what you are. You're prey. If you try to get away now, there will be a shootout. If one side thinks they're losing, they'll shoot you to stop the other side from getting you. Because you're prey. Do you understand?"

It was too much for him. He shook his head. "No."

Then, he looked around like he was looking for an escape.

Time was short, and risk was high. I didn't have time to convince him the right move was to go with us. If he bolted, the fight would start too soon.

So I hit him with an elbow in the temple.

He wasn't expecting it, which made it easier. His brain, full of science and experiments and expert knowledge on isotope separation, smacked against the inside of his skull and went into lockdown.

He teetered on weak knees. Before he could fall, I got behind and put my arms under his.

Farhad's men and the Israelis were still focused on each other, so they didn't see what

I did before it was done.

"Can I get some help?" I asked. The bombmaker wasn't a big man, but I'm mostly average and even a small man is hard to carry alone. "How about one guy from each side?"

Farhad nodded. Esther's boss nodded.

A man from each side grabbed the nuclear bombmaker under each arm and took him to the stairwell.

Chapter 21

Spies and soldiers prioritize different kinds of math.

When you're a soldier, your main kind of math is subtraction. Your objective is to subtract as many soldiers from the other side, whenever and wherever you can. You want to be sure every enemy you meet can never fight again. You want to inflict casualties on the other side.

All else equal, if you subtract enough people from the enemy, you're more likely to win. In the Zero-Sum Game of war, a soldier's objective is to subtract from the other side.

Spies have the same Endgame as soldiers, but the math to get there goes beyond subtraction. A spy's math gets into multinomials and probabilities and layers of games.

A spy's math starts with not subtracting the enemy in front of you. It starts with seeing enemies as someone who might be an addition to your side.

If you can flip an enemy to your side, the math gets more complex and interesting. Because you're not just adding someone who will act for your side. You're also adding someone who can provide you with data and analysis, including data on the decision-making of the other side. You can add awareness about how the other side operates. If you get the right data, you can figure out what they're going to do before they do it. The math goes way beyond subtraction.

Adding an enemy to your side gets you into multiplicative, divisive and exponential effects.

Which is the real reason I wanted Angelo's father to send someone to Wisconsin after me: I wanted the chance to add an enemy to my side. I wanted to recruit an informant in their organization. To win, I needed exponential effects.

And the reason I chose Jake's town for the field of battle was I was more likely to get someone on the fringes of their organization. Geographically distant from the skirmishes in Florida and upstate New York, I was more likely to get someone outside the central power structure. Someone on the fringes is always more likely to be flipped.

But that's only possible if you don't subtract the enemy in front of you.

I jumped out of my car and got behind his. Approaching from the rear driver's side like a cop stopping a DUI, I saw the leather-coated guy had already fallen out of his car.

He was on the shoulder, his hands scrambling in the gravel.

As I closed in on him, I was thinking about how I could flip him. How I could turn him to my side. How I could make him an informant.

But first, I had to stop him from grabbing the gun in his ankle holster and shooting me.

He got to it just as I did, but the button snap slowed him down enough for me to grab his hand. When he brought the weapon up, I twisted it against his grip. His fingers came open, and I pulled the weapon away. If he weren't dazed from the crash and the airbag, it probably would have been harder. But the end result would have been the same: I stood over him with his gun, a Smith and Wesson 360 PD.

He sighed and rolled over. Like it was a moment he had been expecting.

"Are you going kill me?" he asked.

"Probably," I said. "Where are you a cop?"

"City of Chicago," he said.

"Where's your badge?" I asked.

"The console," he said.

I found a leather badge case and grabbed a cell phone miraculously still in its suction-cup holder. On the badge was a circle on a star with the Chicago city seal in the middle. At the bottom was a four-digit badge number. At the top was a bar that said "Sergeant."

On the other side of the badge was an ID. It had a picture of the leather-coated guy in a checkerboard-rimmed cap and uniform. Underneath was a name: Daniel Logenski.

I sighed. "I'd like to not kill you, Daniel. Or is it Dan?"

He didn't answer, so I said, "The problem is that I can't let you go. I can't let you go because you'd go back to the people who sent you and get more guys to come after me. Right?"

He looked up at me and said, "If you kill me, you'll have the Chicago PD and the people who hired me looking for you." He said it in a way that was pro forma. Like he felt like he had to say it, even though he knew it would have no effect.

He was right, but it was a good transition to what I wanted to talk about, so I went with it.

"Killing you would cause problems," I agreed.

"But so would leaving you alive. The same guys would still come after me, whether you're alive or dead. Wouldn't they?"

He didn't say anything.

"I don't want to kill you, and you don't want to die. But I can't let you go, either. A reasonable person, even a jury of twelve of my peers, would probably say I should kill you as a matter of pre-emptive self-defense. But I don't want to."

"Then you don't – You don't have to kill me," he said, with something approaching hope in his eyes.

When you're a spy and you're negotiating, you look to the end and reason backward. Reasoning backward, there's always the chance for what economists call "post-contractual opportunism." Which means the other side can alter the deal after they make it. The other side can do what they shouldn't after the agreement is made.

I had looked to the end and reasoned

backward. I had found a way to be sure he would stick to the deal we were about to make. I had a way to make sure he didn't come back and kill me. But people tend to stick to deals longer if the terms of the deal are their idea.

It was better if he came up with the solution on his own.

I said, "Unless you can think of a way to guarantee you won't come back at me, I'm going to kill you."

Leather-coated Daniel Logenski started thinking.

Chapter 22

We exited the Abu Dhabi mall stairwell in the underground parking garage. Esther's boss must have signaled ahead because the Israelis' four door Mercedes pulled up right away.

With his head swaying, the nuclear bombmaker was pushed into the middle of the backseat. I slid in on one side of him. Farhad got in on the other side. In the front passenger seat went Esther's boss.

The Israeli driver took the ramp up and out of the garage, and the nuclear bombmaker's head fell on my shoulder. Farhad turned around and watched his men fall in behind us. They drove one of the sedans I'd seen at the airport the night before.

Two blocks down, we took a left, then

another turn to the left.

It had only been a minute, but the backseat already stunk. There was sweat from me. There was something coming from the nuclear bombmaker, even though he was still unconscious, either fear or something worse. There was the normal Middle Eastern smell of Farhad and Esther's boss. After two minutes, it was overwhelming.

I opened the window. The desert heat sucked the smells and airconditioned air away.

Heads turned toward me, but nobody said anything. Everyone was thinking about what was coming.

The buildings thinned, and I saw we weren't going toward the mainland. We weren't going across the bridge I'd taken in. And we weren't crossing the other bridges. We were staying on the island, which meant the Israelis were going toward the marina.

Which made sense. The Israelis had probably come by boat so their weapons were easier to get past customs. Easier than a private plane and more anonymous. No tail numbers recorded. Plus, it was easier to get somebody like the nuclear bombmaker out by boat than by plane. By boat they had come and by boat they would leave.

But the fight would be before that. The Israelis would want the fight to be away from their boat. They'd want to keep any gunfire at a distance. Boats and humans are vulnerable to bullet holes in much the same ways.

The Israelis would want to overcome Farhad's men before they reached their boat. Somewhere between where we were and the marina. Where would it be?

The nuclear bombmaker stirred. He lifted his head and looked around. He saw me and startled. He screamed at me in a language I didn't know.

Apparently, Farhad didn't know it either, because he spoke to the nuclear bombmaker in Arabic. "Wataqul alsharikat takun hadiatan."

I didn't know a lot of Arabic, but I recognized the word for "business" or "company." And with "al" in front of it, that meant "the business" or "the company." Which, of course, is what some people call the CIA.

But Farhad didn't know I was CIA, so that was a strange thing to say. It also seemed to confuse the nuclear bombmaker, too, because he switched to a different language to clarify.

"La corporacion?"

We were in the Middle East. I was surrounded by Arabs and Israelis. I was primed for Hebrew and Arabic and English. Not Spanish. But Spanish is what the nuclear bombmaker used.

And Spanish is what Farhad responded with. "La corporacion," Farhad said.

The bombmaker shrank. His face turned white. He stammered in English, "Where are we going?"

But that was a useless question. Esther's boss wasn't going to answer. I didn't know. And

Farhad didn't care.

Farhad said something to the bombmaker in Arabic that I didn't catch.

The bombmaker pulled his seatbelt around and clicked it into place.

A couple of seconds later I knew why.

Chapter 23

There's a myth that you can recruit a source or informant in one meeting. That you can find some single point of leverage, and they'll become your source. That you can threaten them, and they'll do what you want.

Not true for ninety percent of humanity. And the other ten percent usually isn't worth it.

Leather-coated Daniel Logenski wasn't one of that ten percent. First, because he was worth flipping. And second, because he wasn't going to flip in one meeting. He wasn't going to turn to my side after our first encounter.

Maybe, if I had a weekend with him. Maybe, if I could offer him a million dollars and his own island.

But even that was unlikely.

Because every relationship requires reciprocity, like Sarah said. Reciprocity is back and forth. Reciprocity is exchange. Reciprocity requires more than one meeting. Reciprocity takes time. Reciprocity means a spy's first encounter with an enemy isn't like a soldier's.

When you're a spy, you're not trying to figure out the best way to eliminate the enemy. You're trying to figure out a way to flip them. Which means the first encounter with an enemy is the first opportunity to start the back and forth of reciprocity.

When I said, "Unless you can think of a way to guarantee you won't come back at me, I'm going to kill you," I was compressing reciprocity into an offer.

I was offering not to kill him, if he came up with something. It was an offer, but he would need to fill in the details of the offer for me not to kill him. So, reciprocity. An exchange. A basis for the future.

Daniel Logenski said, "I don't know, man. I

don't know what I can do for you."

Which wasn't an offer, so I lifted the gun.

He raised his hands over his face. "Ok, ok. If you let me go, I promise not to tell them you're alive."

"That doesn't do it for me," I said. "Because you can change your mind as soon as you're gone. Post-contractual opportunism. It's maybe a five percent chance you keep that promise. If I kill you, it's 100 percent you don't tell them I'm alive."

A thought flickered across Logenski's face. "But if you kill me, they'll know you're alive for sure. One hundred percent."

Logenski saw that he had some bargaining power, which was good. It meant he was more confident a deal would be made. Hope was back in his eyes. His mind was racing.

I decided to help him out. "That's why I don't want to kill you. But how do we raise the chance you don't tell them I'm alive?"

This was going to be the hard part of the

negotiation. Logenski was going to need to accept the possibility of a future loss. Which meant he was going to go through the Kubler-Ross five stages of grief. He was going to go from denial all the way to acceptance. Which is hard for anyone to do quickly.

Logenski didn't say anything, so I decided to help him out again. "What's the name of Angelo's father?"

He didn't answer.

"You've got to give me something," I said. "If you're going to live, you've got to give me something."

Logenski did something I didn't expect: He laughed. "Ok – Here's something: You've got it all wrong, man. It's not Angelo's father running the show. It's his grandmother. We call her Bueli."

Chapter 24

The police in the U.S. have something called the "Precision Immobilization Technique" or "tactical ramming." They're trained to use it in a car chase when the car is going toward a populated area or could crash into other cars on the road or put bystanders in danger.

The way the police are trained to use it, the car isn't supposed to flip. The police pull up to the side of the target vehicle and ease to the side. After making contact, the police steer into the target vehicle and push until the target car's rear wheels lose traction. When the rear wheels lose traction, the car skids to the side. The driver loses control. If the police did it right, the car comes to rest on a shoulder or landing area and no one gets hurt.

But the police are only supposed to use it if everybody is going less than thirty-five miles per hour. At higher speeds, the dynamics change.

The dynamics change because there's a point after the car is nudged to the side when the wheels that didn't have traction stick to the road again. But when they stick, the momentum of the vehicle is no longer going forward. It's going side-to-side.

At fifty miles per hour or greater when wheels stick, all that side-to-side momentum pushes against that sticking wheel. If the outside wheel sticks first, there's trouble.

The center of gravity, normally in the middle of the car, shifts toward the sticking wheel and over.

The car flips.

That's what Daniel Logenski had been trying to do when he hit me in Wisconsin.

And that's what Farhad's men did when they hit the Israeli car on the side.

When he felt the rear wheels lose traction, the Israeli driver steered into the turn.

But we were going too fast. The outside wheel stuck, and the side-to-side momentum took us into a flip.

That's when my training took over.

When a car flips, the first things to watch out for are the loose things. A coffee mug can destroy your cheekbone. A cell phone can break your teeth. A coin can take out your eye.

After the loose things, you watch out for your arms.

Most people think your body is most at risk, but it's not. Centrifugal force pushes your body into your seat. As the car flips, the force pushes you deeper into your seat.

But your arms are a different story. Centrifugal force takes your arms wide when the car flips. They'll fly away from your body and hit everything there is to hit. Only hard things will stop them from moving.

If you've got the window open, it's worse.

Your arms will go out the window. If that happens, they could get crushed in the rollover.

Which is why my training said: If your car flips and you're in the driver's seat, grab the wheel. Hold on tight until the car stops moving.

But I wasn't in the driver's seat of the Israeli car, so I defaulted to the next best thing: I grabbed the waist strap of my seatbelt.

I don't know how many times we flipped. When the car stopped, I was in a daze. I couldn't think straight. The world was still spinning.

I remember Farhad and the bombmaker got out of the car on the other side. The Israeli driver was moving, then his head fell forward like he'd been shot. And a bullet whizzed through the broken window next to me.

There were pops of gunshots as I rolled out of the car through my mangled door. The other Israeli car was coming toward us. Esther's boss was already out. He was standing next to the upside-down wheel still spinning. He had a bucking pistol in his hand. He was firing at the car that had rammed us.

Farhad's car was going in reverse and was already thirty yards away. An Israeli bullet shattered the windshield, but it kept going backward. A few seconds later, it spun around and accelerated.

I watched myself from a distance as the Israelis went to work.

They got their unconscious driver and Esther's boss to their second car. Then, one of them pulled the pin on a phosphorous grenade and looked at me.

I stumbled back from the car.

He threw the grenade in the car. The car went up in flames.

The Israelis drove away, and I was alone on an Abu Dhabi road next to a burning car.

I got to my feet and staggered back the way we came. After ten minutes, a taxi passed by, and I took it to my hotel.

And that was it.

Nothing more to do in Abu Dhabi, so I left on the next flight out.

I thought I'd never see Farhad, the bombmaker or Esther again.

I was wrong.

Chapter 25

When Daniel Logenski told me Angelo's grandmother was running the show, I didn't expect it. Which was good.

It was good because it meant Logenski probably wasn't lying. Or, if he was lying, it was an elaborate lie. Which would be unusual because an elaborate lie requires a lot of cognitive ability. Cognitive ability most people don't have. Even fewer have it when they've just been hit with an airbag.

If he wanted to lie, Logenski would have tried an easy lie, not an elaborate lie. An easy lie would have been to let me keep thinking that Angelo's father was running the show. An easy lie would have been to give me a Hispanic-sounding male name when I asked about Angelo's father. An easy lie would have led me down the road I was already on.

But Logenski didn't take me down that road. He corrected me, which was good. It meant he probably wasn't lying.

If he wasn't lying, he saw a future ahead. If he wasn't lying, it was because he thought some reciprocity was coming. If so, he didn't want to start our relationship with a lie.

To keep the reciprocity going, I tossed Logenski his badge. It skittered across the gravel, flipped over and hit his knee.

He picked it up and put it inside his leather coat.

We needed more things to exchange, so I pulled out the phone I had grabbed from the suction cup holder. When I raised it, tiny gyroscopes inside triggered the lock screen. The background picture showed two little girls.

"Daughters or nieces?" I asked.

He didn't want to answer, but information like that was part of the reciprocity we were establishing. It was a test, and he knew it. So he said, "Nieces."

"Where's the other phone?" I asked.

He started to ask, "What other phone?" But he stopped himself because even though a question can't be a lie, playing dumb wasn't being honest. He wanted to be honest, so he didn't ask the question.

I answered the question he didn't ask. "The phone you use to call Angelo's grandmother. No way you call her from a phone with your nieces' picture on it. You're a cop and too smart for that."

Logenski sighed and pulled a flip phone out of his jacket pocket.

The flip phone didn't have anybody's picture on it. It was dull and gray with a dull, gray brand on it.

The next thing Logenski was going to do would have been better if he had thought of it on his own. But we were running out of time. At any moment, someone could drive by and ask questions about why two banged-up cars were splayed across the shoulder.

"What do you want me to do?" he asked.

I said, "I want you to call Angelo's grandmother. Put her on speaker, so I can hear you tell her you killed me."

Which would result in two things, if he did it. It would make him lie on my behalf, and it would prove he hadn't been lying about Angelo's grandmother being in charge.

Logenski thought about my offer.

To hurry him up, I said, "You're going to have to do something you don't like before you leave. Some of those things involve pain and suffering, like a gunshot to the knee. Some of those things involve putting other people at risk, like the parents of your nieces. All things considered, this is the best. And the easiest."

As I said that, headlights bounced down the road behind me. A car came toward us.

The car slowed. The window came down. "You guys all right?" asked an old man in an old hat.

"He's a little banged up, but I'm fine," I said. "Damn deer jumped out right in front of me. He rear-ended me."

The old man compared my story to the damage he could see. "You need me to call for help?" he asked.

"Already did," I said. "They're on the way."

"All right," said the old man. He rolled up his window and drove away slowly. Slow enough that he could have been fishing out his phone to make a call.

I turned back to Logenski. "He's probably dialing 911 right now. Which means we've got between eight and twelve minutes. In that time, you can be dead or you can be in your car and two miles away."

Because he was a cop, he checked my response time math in his head and nodded. "I'll call Bueli."

Chapter 26

When I told my boss what happened in Abu Dhabi, his first question wasn't about whether I was hurt. It wasn't about whether I'd been shot or got a concussion or had any stress fractures. His first question was, "Were you compromised?"

My boss was short and skinny and joined the Hash House Harriers wherever he was posted. He liked to run, but he also liked to drink beer, so the semi-British HHH with its running courses between pubs was the perfect fit. I don't know if he had a lot of energy because he ran or he ran because he had a lot of energy, but he was intense. And reflective. Which meant he usually asked good questions. And he asked them in the right order.

"No," I said. "Farhad and the Israelis know my face and the Israelis know my alias, but nobody knows my true name."

My boss nodded. "Were you hurt?"

"My elbow hit something when the car flipped, but it's just bruised," I said.

He smiled. "You want worker's comp?" A joke, because spies in flipped cars and shootouts don't submit paperwork for worker's compensation. That's for bureaucrats who slip on stairs.

"No," I said.

He smiled again. "Then you have two options: You can write up everything that happened, including Farhad and the Israelis. You'll be sent back to headquarters to sit on a desk for six months, maybe a year. They'll try to decide whether you're compromised based on no new information. But you're not compromised, which you already know. And I already know. So, you can take the second option: write up the meeting with the bombmaker and say you didn't see an avenue to recruitment and close the file and leave out the rest."

It was early in my career, and I didn't know what to do. I didn't know if my boss was testing me. If he wanted me to write up the whole thing because that's what I should do, or if he wanted me to take the second option so I could stay in the field. Or, if he wanted me to take the second option so he'd keep me in the field and have leverage over me, which is the kind of bullshit some spy bosses do.

But I didn't think my boss was trying to gain leverage over me. He didn't care about that. What he cared about was losing one of his spies to headquarters. He didn't want me sitting on a desk thousands of miles away when I could be doing work for him. He wanted me in the field as much as I wanted to be.

I took the second option.

In my report on Abu Dhabi, I didn't write about Farhad. I didn't write about Esther or the rest of the Israelis. Which meant I also didn't write about the confrontation in the mall and the Israeli car flipping and the shootout and Farhad and the bombmaker getting away.

I didn't write about any of that and stayed in the field. Zach Middleton and all his documents died in a burn bag, and I was reborn with a sixth name. A sixth name unconnected to me or the CIA by resemblance, contiguity of time and place or cause and effect. A sixth name David Hume nor anybody else could connect to me.

In the long run, not reporting contact with enemies and quasi-allies will catch up to you, like it did to me. But the long run is made up of short runs. In the short run, I wanted to get back in the field. So I left them out of my report.

Because I left them out of my report, I didn't get the benefit of someone at headquarters reading it and explaining to me why the bombmaker called "Al-sharika" "La corporacion" instead of "La compañia." It was something somebody with some expertise in Latin America would have known. Somebody like Jake.

But I didn't know much about Latin America, so I didn't know the difference.

Which means I didn't know the difference mattered.

I didn't know the difference mattered until I talked to Daniel Logenski in Wisconsin.

Chapter 27

Before Logenski called Angelo's grandmother, we went over the questions she would ask and how Logenski should answer.

Then he called her.

She didn't pick up.

Logenski said, "She'll probably call back in a minute."

Which gave us time to go over the questions again.

Then Logenski's flip phone rang. A blue number appeared on the outside screen.

He flipped open the phone and pressed the speaker button.

A smoky, raspy female voice said, "It's done?"

Logenski said, "Yes."

"Who was he?"

"Ex-military guy who liked to pick fights. Him and the other guy in New York. Nothing more than that. No organization. No connections. Just two jackasses trying to be tough guys."

"Where's the other guy from New York?"

"Dead."

"Dead how?" said the voice from far away.

Logenski paused because it wasn't a question we'd discussed. "This guy didn't say. Maybe from the fight. I don't know."

"How did he find Angelo in Florida?"

"Dumb luck, he said, and I believe him. This guy wasn't very smart, and he wasn't going to live long. He was running around picking fights until someone killed him."

"He didn't know anything more?"

"No, ma'am."

There was a pause on the other end. "Good job. Compensation will be waiting." There was a click. The blue number on the inside screen pulsed like a heartbeat, then disappeared.

Logenski flipped the phone closed and looked at me expectantly.

He had done what I asked him to do. Now, it was time to do what I'd promised to do: Let him go.

Reciprocity.

Before I let him go, I could have asked more questions about why the Cubans had been in upstate New York. About why they were using the weapons of Quebecois separatists. About why they panicked and killed Bill, the gun range owner. But I was going to get the answers from the people who had been there soon enough, so I didn't bother.

Instead, I asked him another question: "Does her organization have a name? What do they call themselves?"

He answered with a name I'd heard before. "The Corporation."

My thoughts accelerated down the same path they went down in Abu Dhabi. It was a path of misunderstanding. Of cognitive bias.

Because I'd heard my own organization called "The Company" so many times.

"The Company?" I asked.

"No," he said. "The Corporation."

"Where's Angelo's grandmother?" I asked.

"You don't want to go there," he said.

"Where is she?" I repeated.

"Union City, New Jersey," he said.

"Give me the password to your personal phone," I said.

Logenski told me the four-digit code, and I opened the phone. Past the lock screen of his nieces, I looked at his social media profiles, then found the number of his phone. I memorized the number and handed it back to him.

"Before I call you, I'll text you one word: Chicago. When you see that text from a phone you don't know, answer when that number calls you next. Got it?"

Logenski nodded. "What now?"

"You can go," I said.

"I can go?" he asked.

"You can go," I repeated.

As Daniel Logenski drove away, I wondered how long it would be before I killed him.

Chapter 28

The next morning, it took me ten minutes to find the right tree branch in Jake's yard. It needed to be:

1. Big enough to cover both bullet holes in the rear windshield and;
2. Small enough to control on the downswing.

I found the right tree branch on the far side of Jake's house and dragged it across the gravel driveway. I lifted it over my head and smashed the rear window of Jake's car.

The rest of the damage was along the bumper and side. It had been done by metal, which most people would assume would be another car. There were no tree branch adjustments to be made, but that didn't matter as much as the bullet holes. Bullet holes meant the police would be called. Bullet holes meant more questions.

To avoid as many questions as possible, I called Sarah for help.

"You said you were going to call in a few days. Now, you're calling sooner," she said. "Do you like me or something?"

That stopped me. "Of course. You're great," I said.

"Great?" she repeated. "Great?"

"Yeah. You're great. My car got beat up last night. It needs some body and bumper work. Do you know anybody who does that kind of work and won't ask questions?"

"I don't know," she said. "I don't know where this is going."

"Where what's going?" I asked.

"Okay," she said. "Here it is: All the guys around here are losers. You're not from around here, and I don't think you're a loser."

"I won't be around much longer," I said. "But I'll take you to lunch, if you can give me the name of somebody who does auto body work and won't ask questions."

"Questions about what?"

"About why it's banged up."

"My brother has a shop downtown."

"Which brother?"

"Ed, from last night," she said.

"He won't ask questions?"

She was offended. "Not about the car. After all, he told you to take care of it. But he might ask other questions."

"What other questions?"

She went an octave up. "Questions about your intentions. With me."

"My intention is singular, not plural. It's only to take you to lunch," I said.

"Hmmm," she said. "He's not going to like that."

She was right.

When I dropped off Jake's car at Ed's auto body shop, he asked, "Why are you hanging out with my sister?"

"She's great, but I'm leaving town again soon. We're just having lunch, then I'm gone."

"How long are you gone?"

"Don't know," I said, and all Ed did was nod.

At lunch, Sarah asked again a different version of the same question. "What do you want to do? With me?"

When she asked that, a whole future opened up in front of me. A future sitting on the deck and looking over the lake. A future watching fish break the surface and fog rise from cattails. A future with Sarah.

But there was a problem with that future: Me.

I don't know exactly where or when I became what I am. Somewhere between my sixteenth and twenty-first name, maybe.

That's when fighting with game theory, structured thinking, probability and physics became more than a job. More than a set of objectives. More than anything else I loved.

When I left the CIA, I tried to forget it. I tried to walk away. And I got soft. When Jake brought me back, I was back in the game. I was back doing what I should because of who I am. Doing what I couldn't walk away from again.

I didn't know it until Sarah.

Sarah repeated her question. "What do you want to do?"

"I don't think it's going to work out," I said.

"Why not?" She was mystified.

"Because I travel too much."

She shrugged. "Why not come back and see? Before you throw in the towel, take me out to dinner and see."

Which I could do, if I made through what was about to happen. If I was still alive. So I said, "Okay. Dinner when I come back."

"Will it be my turn to pay? Or will we be past that?" she asked.

"We'll see what happens," I said.

Sarah smiled, which would make anyone want to stay. Even someone who had to be somewhere else.

I paid for lunch, and Sarah drove me back to Jake's house. She said she'd get Jake's car back into his garage after Ed fixed it. And she'd keep things clean while I was gone.

I got into the rental car in Jake's garage and left town.

The next afternoon, I pulled into Union City, New Jersey and started looking for nodes, strands and Angelo's grandmother.

If you enjoyed *The 24th Name, Part II*, please let a friend know.

For updates on next books, join John's email list at:

www.spysguide.com

More by John Braddock:

Fiction:

The 24th Name

The Adventures of Young John Quincy Adams: Sea Chase

Non-fiction:

A Spy's Guide To Thinking

A Spy's Guide To Strategy

Made in the USA
Monee, IL
02 October 2020